Bea and the Dance Show

T0364520

Written by Rebecca Adlard

Illustrated by Valentina Pieralli

Collins

Who's in this story?

Listen and say

Miss Dint

Kitty

🎧 Miss Dint, the dance teacher, said, "And one and two and three and four! And one and two and three and four. Listen to the music."

4

The children danced. It was a new dance and it was very difficult.

I can't do it!

Miss Dint said, "Stop. Let's try again."

Kitty said, "I can do it, Miss Dint. I can show everyone."

7

Miss Dint played the music. She said, "Watch Kitty." The children sat down and watched. Kitty danced. She was good. They clapped.

Thank you, Kitty.

Well done, Kitty!

That was very good!

8

Miss Dint said, "Let's try again. And one and two and three and four! Listen to the music. Watch Kitty."

The children danced again. They watched Kitty. The dance was better.

In the next dance class, Miss Dint showed the children a poster.

Spring Dance Show

20 March 2:00 p.m.

School

"A dance show?" said Bea. "I don't like shows."

"Shows are fun," said Kitty. "Our dance is good now."

"I don't want to dance in a show," said Bea.

"It's OK, Bea," said Miss Dint. "You can watch and help me."

Bea watched the others.
She helped
Miss Dint.

She put on the music ...

...and she made
the clothes for
the dance show.

"Stop!" said Miss Dint. "I don't like this part of the dance."

"Let's turn around," said Kitty.

"Or, kick your right legs and then your left legs and then turn around," said Bea.

14

"That's a very good idea, Bea," said
Miss Dint. "Let's try everyone!"

The group tried Bea's idea. It was a good
idea. Everyone liked it.

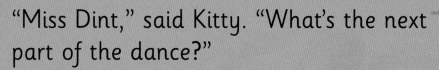

"Miss Dint," said Kitty. "What's the next part of the dance?"

"Wait a minute, Kitty," said Miss Dint.

"I know what it is," said Bea. "You do this."

"Oh yes!" said Liam.

On Friday, after the class, Miss Dint fell.
She was hurt.

Miss Dint could not come to the
dance class.

"What do we do?" asked Liam.

"I want to do the dance show," said Suzi.

"Bea can be our dance teacher," said Kitty. "She knows the dance, the music and the clothes."

"Please Bea!" said the children.

"Is my hair OK, Bea?" asked Suzi.

"Can you help me with my clothes, Bea?" asked Liam.

"When do we kick our legs to the right?" asked Flo.

Bea helped everyone.

Bea watched her friends dance.
They were great!

"You were very good," said the judge. "Where is your dance teacher?"

Kitty said, "Bea, come here."

"Oh," said the judge.

They gave Bea some flowers.

"I like dance shows," said Bea.

Picture dictionary

Listen and repeat

dance class

dance show

dance teacher

judge

poster

turn around

1 Look and order the story

2 Listen and say

Collins

Published by Collins
An imprint of HarperCollins*Publishers*
Westerhill Road
Bishopbriggs
Glasgow
G64 2QT

HarperCollins*Publishers*
1st Floor, Watermarque Building
Ringsend Road
Dublin 4
Ireland

William Collins' dream of knowledge for all began with the publication of his first book in 1819.

A self-educated mill worker, he not only enriched millions of lives, but also founded a flourishing publishing house. Today, staying true to this spirit, Collins books are packed with inspiration, innovation and practical expertise. They place you at the centre of a world of possibility and give you exactly what you need to explore it.

© HarperCollins*Publishers* Limited 2020

10 9 8 7 6 5 4 3 2

ISBN 978-0-00-839826-2

Collins® and COBUILD® are registered trademarks of HarperCollins*Publishers* Limited

www.collins.co.uk/elt

British Library Cataloguing in Publication Data

A catalogue record for this publication is available from the British Library.

Author: Rebecca Adlard
Illustrator: Valentina Pieralli (Beehive)
Series editor: Rebecca Adlard
Publishing manager: Lisa Todd
Product managers: Jennifer Hall and Caroline Green
In-house editor: Alma Puts Keren
Project manager: Emily Hooton
Editor: Rebecca Adlard
Proofreaders: Natalie Murray and Michael Lamb
Cover designer: Kevin Robbins
Typesetter: 2Hoots Publishing Services Ltd
Audio produced by id audio, London
Reading guide author: Emma Wilkinson
Production controller: Rachel Weaver
Printed and bound by: GPS Group, Slovenia

MIX
Paper from
responsible sources

FSC www.fsc.org **FSC™ C007454**

This book is produced from independently certified FSC™ paper to ensure responsible forest management.

For more information visit: **www.harpercollins.co.uk/green**

Download the audio for this book and a reading guide for parents and teachers at www.collins.co.uk/839826